STAR WARS®

Read-Along STORYBOOK AND CD
TREASURY

CONTENTS

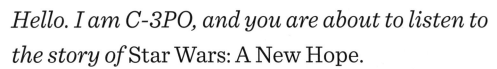

Hello. I am C-3PO, and you are about to listen to the story of Star Wars: A New Hope.

You can also read along with the story in your book. Unless you are already programmed to know when the pages end, you will know it is time to turn the page when you hear this sound. . . .

I believe the storyteller is ready, so let us begin.

A long time ago in a galaxy far, far away. . . .

Read-Along Story Produced by Randy Thornton and Ted Kryczko;
Co-produced and Engineered by Jeff Sheridan; Adapted by Randy Thornton; Illustrated by Brian Rood.
Ⓟ 2015 Walt Disney Records/Lucasfilm Ltd. © & TM 2015 Lucasfilm Ltd. All rights reserved.

THERE WAS A PERIOD OF CIVIL WAR. Rebel spaceships fighting for freedom had won their first victory against the evil Galactic Empire. During the battle, rebel spies managed to steal secret design plans to the Empire's ultimate weapon, the Death Star—an armored space station with enough power to destroy an entire planet. Pursued by the Empire's agents, Princess Leia of Alderaan raced home aboard her rebel starship, carrying the plans that could save her people.

Suddenly, a laser blast rocked Princess Leia's starship. Inside, two droids—C-3PO and R2-D2—tried to steady themselves. The larger of the two, C-3PO, turned to his small counterpart, R2-D2. "We'll be destroyed for sure. This is madness!"

The starship began to shake, straining against an invisible force. It was caught in the tractor beam of an Imperial Star Destroyer, and was being pulled into a docking bay.

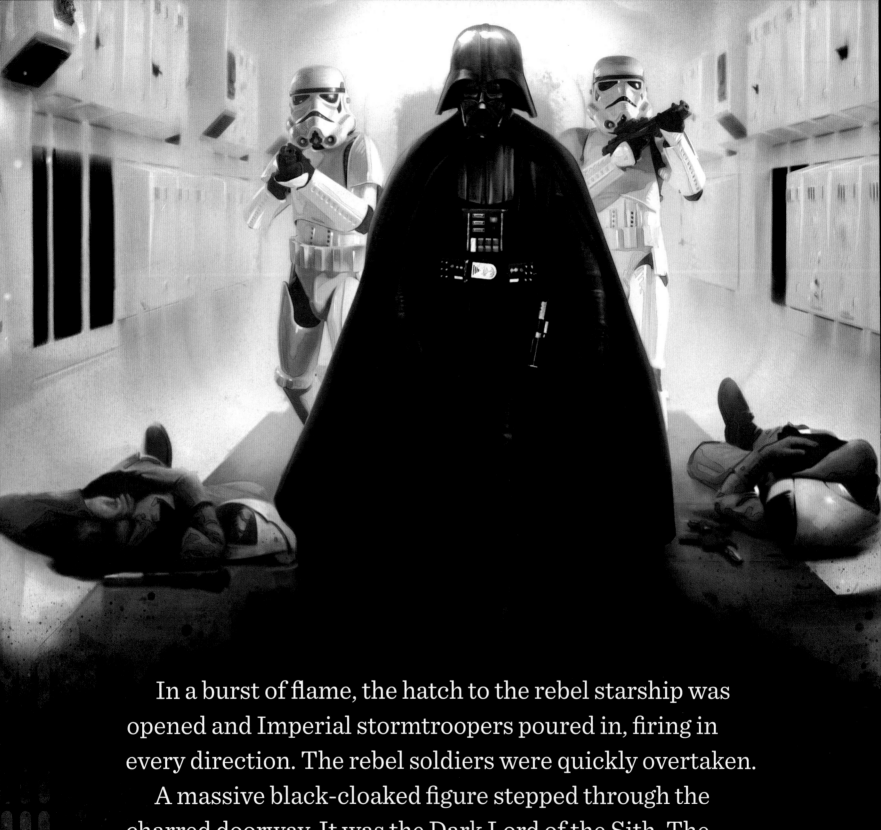

In a burst of flame, the hatch to the rebel starship was opened and Imperial stormtroopers poured in, firing in every direction. The rebel soldiers were quickly overtaken.

A massive black-cloaked figure stepped through the charred doorway. It was the Dark Lord of the Sith. The feared Darth Vader.

In another part of the ship, C-3PO was looking for R2-D2, whom he'd lost during the attack. Following the familiar sound of his friend, C-3PO came across a beautiful woman kneeling in front of the little droid. She turned and quickly slipped into the shadows.

"There you are. Where have you been? Mission? What mission?" C-3PO followed the little droid as he entered an escape pod.

"I'm going to regret this." The pod burst from the ship and headed for Tatooine, the planet below.

Within moments, Princess Leia was captured and brought before the Dark Lord. "Darth Vader. Only you could be so bold."

"Don't act so surprised, Your Highness. You weren't on any mercy mission this time. Several transmissions were beamed to this ship by rebel spies. I want to know what happened to the plans they sent you."

"I'm a member of the Imperial Senate on a diplomatic mission to Alderaan—"

"You are part of the Rebel Alliance and a traitor. Take her away!"

On the desert planet of Tatooine, C-3PO and R2-D2's escape pod had landed. No sooner had they disembarked than they were captured by the Jawas, a group of little hooded creatures. "We're doomed. Do you think they'll melt us down?"

Scavengers by nature, the Jawas claimed the droids as their own and sold them to Owen Lars, a moisture farmer and guardian of Luke Skywalker. "Luke, take these two over to the garage, will you? I want you to have both of these cleaned up before dinner."

As C-3PO was lowered into an oil bath, Luke began to clean the little R2 unit. "You got a lot of carbon scoring here. It looks like you boys have seen a lot of action."

"With all we've been through, sometimes I'm amazed we're in as good condition as we are, what with the Rebellion and all."

"You know of the Rebellion against the Empire?"

"That's how we came to be in your service, if you take my meaning, sir."

Excited by this link to the Rebellion, Luke turned back to R2-D2 and discovered an object in his head rotation joint. "Well, my little friend, you've got something jammed in here real good. Were you on a starcruiser or a—"

There was a flash of light, and suddenly R2-D2 began projecting a holographic image of Princess Leia into the center of the room. "Help me, Obi-Wan Kenobi. You're my only hope."

Luke sat there, dazzled. "Who is she? She's beautiful."

The stubborn R2 unit refused to play back the entire message. C-3PO interpreted the little droid's mechanical beeps for Luke.

"He says that he's the property of Obi-Wan Kenobi, a resident of these parts. And it's a private message for him."

"I wonder if he means old Ben Kenobi."

"I beg your pardon, sir, but do you know what he's talking about?"

"Well, I don't know anyone named Obi-Wan, but old Ben lives out beyond the Dune Sea. He's kind of a strange old hermit."

Fearing that the droids may have been stolen, Luke set off to deliver them to Ben Kenobi, along with the secret message.

Luke presented Ben with the droids. "I saw part of a message R2-D2 was—"

"I seem to have found it."

"General Kenobi, years ago you served my father in the Clone Wars. Now he begs you to help him in his struggle against the Empire. I have placed information vital to the survival of the Rebellion into the memory systems of this R2 unit. You must see this droid safely delivered to him on Alderaan. This is our most desperate hour. Help me, Obi-Wan Kenobi. You're my only hope."

Ben turned to Luke. "I was once a Jedi Knight, like your father."

"My father was a Jedi?"

"Yes . . . and this was his lightsaber." Ben handed Luke the sword. "He wanted you to have it when you were old enough. You should learn the ways of the Force if you're to come with me to Alderaan."

"I can't leave here. I'll take you as far as Anchorhead."

"You must do what you feel is right, of course."

On their way to Anchorhead, Luke, Ben, and the droids came across the Jawa sandcrawler, destroyed by Imperial troops.

"If they traced the robots here, they may have learned who they sold them to. And that would lead them back . . . home!"

"Wait, Luke. It's too dangerous."

But Luke was already in his landspeeder and gone. When he arrived at the farm, he was devastated to find all that he had ever known destroyed and smoldering.

Sadly, he returned to Ben. "I want to come with you to Alderaan. There's nothing here for me now. I want to learn the ways of the Force and become a Jedi like my father."

Though their destination was clear, they still needed a ship and a pilot to take them there. The best place to find a pilot was the Mos Eisley Cantina, home to a strange assortment of creatures from throughout the galaxy. Ben took Luke around and made some introductions.

"Chewbacca here. He's first mate on a ship that might suit us."

The tall Wookiee led them to a table off in the corner where they met a rough-looking star pilot. "Han Solo. I'm the captain of the *Millennium Falcon*. You guys got yourself a ship. We'll leave as soon as you're ready. Docking bay ninety-four."

While Luke and Ben set off to sell the landspeeder for some extra money, Han returned to his ship only to be met by the hideous gangster Jabba the Hutt. The vicious Hutt demanded the money that Han owed him. The captain tried to gain some time. "I got a nice easy charter now. Pay you back plus a little extra."

Jabba agreed but he made it clear that if Han failed again, he would put such a high price on his head that he wouldn't be able to go anywhere without an army of bounty hunters waiting to collect it.

The *Millennium Falcon* took off, racing toward Alderaan. Meanwhile, at Alderaan, the Death Star had just entered orbit. On board, Darth Vader was taking the princess to the commander of the space station.

"Princess Leia, before your execution, I would like you to be my first guest at a ceremony that will make this battle station fully operational. No star system will dare oppose the Emperor now."

He turned to the technician. "You may fire when ready."
A beam of light shot out of the Death Star, and the planet
Alderaan exploded in a tremendous fireball.

At the same moment, the *Millennium Falcon* came out
of hyperspace and was suddenly pelted with debris from
the destroyed planet. The only thing seemingly intact was
a small moon nearby.

"That's no moon. That's a space station." Ben was right.

Suddenly the ship shook violently. Han grabbed the controls. "We're caught in a tractor beam! They're pulling us in!"

When the *Falcon* docked, the Imperial search crew jumped on board. But they found the ship empty. Shaking their heads in disbelief, they left. Han—along with the others—emerged from secret compartments, and climbed aboard the Death Star.

While Ben set off to deactivate the tractor beam, R2 plugged into a Death Star computer and discovered that Princess Leia was aboard. Luke persuaded Han and Chewbacca to help him rescue her. They knocked out some guards, took their uniforms, and disguised themselves as stormtroopers escorting their prisoner, Chewbacca.

Once inside the detention block, they located Leia's
cell. She was startled as her door opened and an unusual
stormtrooper entered.

"I'm Luke Skywalker. I'm here to rescue you. I've got

Suddenly, lasers were exploding around them. The Imperial troops had our heroes completely covered. They forced them down a hallway with no means of escape.

"This is some rescue. When you came in here, didn't you have a plan for getting out?" The princess grabbed Luke's blaster and ripped open a hole in the wall. "Into the garbage chute, flyboy!"

One by one they all dove into the hole, landing safely in a huge garbage bin.

Without warning, the walls began to close in on them. They'd landed in a trash compactor! It took all their strength to keep the four sides from crushing them, and for a while it didn't look good.

Then Luke suddenly remembered the droids. He contacted them on his comlink, and instructed R2 to shut down all the garbage mashers. Everyone escaped with barely a scratch.

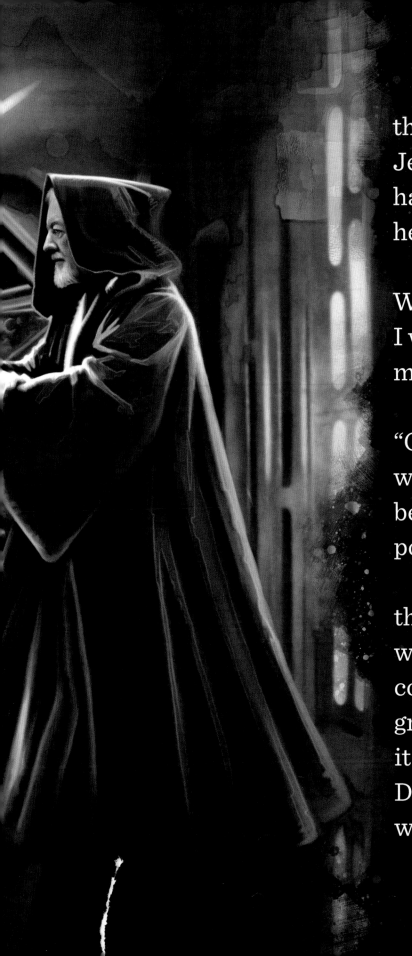

Meanwhile, Ben had deactivated the tractor beam. Stealthily, the old Jedi made his way back through the hallways to the *Falcon*, when suddenly he felt the presence of the Dark Lord.

"I've been waiting for you, Obi-Wan. We meet again at last. When I left you, I was but the learner; now I am the master." On went his lightsaber.

Ben quickly ignited his sword, too. "Only a master of evil, Darth. You can't win. If you strike me down, I shall become more powerful than you can possibly imagine."

Luke and his friends arrived at the docking bay, where the *Falcon* was in sight. But there was a strange commotion going on at one end, and a group of stormtroopers were watching it closely. It was the battle between the Dark Lord and Obi-Wan Kenobi. Vader would swing and Ben would block.

But when the old Jedi saw Luke, a serene look came over him. He stopped fighting, closed his eyes, and raised his sword to his face. Vader swept his lightsaber through Obi-Wan's cloak, but suddenly he was gone. Only his robes, in a crumpled heap, remained.

Luke was horrified. "NO!"

The stormtroopers spun around and opened fire. Leia and the droids raced to the ship as Han, Chewbacca, and Luke fired back.

Within seconds, the *Millennium Falcon* shot out of the docking bay. But it was not alone. Four Imperial TIE fighters were hot on its trail. Han showed Luke the gunports. "Come on, buddy, we're not out of this yet."

The attack was severe, but our young heroes won. Afterward, they arrived at Rebel Headquarters with the Death Star plans.

But Darth Vader had placed a homing beacon aboard the *Millennium Falcon,* and the Imperial Death Star was approaching. Using the secret plan, the rebels launched their ships and headed straight for the Death Star.

They zoomed across the surface of the space station as enemy laser cannons fired back. It soon became obvious that the Imperial troops had to fight the rebels ship-to-ship. Waves of TIE fighters screamed out of the Death Star and attacked. Even Darth Vader himself manned a fighter.

The Empire was gaining ground. One rebel pilot had failed to hit the weak spot of the space station. Now it was up to Luke. But Vader was right on Luke's heels. "The Force is strong with this one." As Vader was about to fire, a lasershot ripped past him and hit his wingman. The explosion sent Vader's ship spinning into space.

"Yahoo! You're clear, kid. Let's blow this thing and go home." It was Han!

As Luke raced to hit the target, he heard Ben's voice. "Use the Force, Luke." Luke fired two proton torpedoes at the Death Star. It was a direct hit. The rebel ships raced into hyperspace just as the space station exploded in a tremendous flash.

With the destruction of the Death Star, the rebels had won one of their great victories over the Empire. Hundreds of rebel troops gathered together to honor Han Solo and Luke Skywalker for their heroic deeds during the battle. Princess Leia awarded the two men with medals of valor as the crowd cheered their triumph. Through the happiness, however, the rebels knew that, though the dreaded Death Star had been destroyed, the Empire, the Emperor, and Darth Vader were still in power and a threat to freedom. But all that would have to wait until the next adventure. . . .

THE EMPIRE STRIKES BACK

Read-Along
STORYBOOK AND CD

Hello. I am C-3PO, and you are about to listen to the story of Star Wars: The Empire Strikes Back.

You can also read along with the story in your book. Unless you are already programmed to know when the pages end, you will know it is time to turn the page when you hear this sound....

I believe the storyteller is ready, so let us begin.

A long time ago in a galaxy far, far away....

Read-Along Story Produced by Randy Thornton and Ted Kryczko;
Co-produced and Engineered by Jeff Sheridan; Adapted by Randy Thornton; Illustrated by Brian Rood.

IT WAS A DARK TIME FOR THE REBEL ALLIANCE. Although the Death Star had been destroyed, the Imperial troops still had managed to force the rebels out of their hidden base and pursue them across the galaxy. A group of freedom fighters led by Luke Skywalker had established a new secret base on the remote ice world of Hoth. The evil lord Darth Vader, obsessed with finding young Skywalker, had dispatched thousands of probes into the far reaches of space.

Trotting his tauntaun across the tundra, Luke reported in on a routine scouting mission. "There's a meteorite that hit the ground near here. I want to check it out. It won't take long."

Suddenly, a vicious snow beast knocked Luke off his mount. The wampa dragged the unconscious rebel into its icy cave.

When Luke woke up, he realized he was about to become the wampa's next meal. As the snow beast approached, he surprised it with a swing of his lightsaber and scrambled out of the cave.

But outside, his tauntaun had been killed by the snow beast, and a blizzard was raging, making it difficult to see. Then he heard a familiar voice. "Luke, you will go to the Dagobah system. There you will learn from Yoda, the Jedi Master who instructed me."

Exhausted, Luke collapsed into a snowdrift. Fortunately, Han Solo was nearby. He rescued the young Jedi, put up a shelter against the cold night air, and by the next morning, they were rescued.

While Luke recovered in the medical center, Han and Chewbacca were alerted to an unusual signal coming from outside the camp. They went to investigate and found an Imperial probe droid. Han radioed back to the base. "It's a good bet the Empire knows we're here." The rebels began evacuating immediately.

Aboard Darth Vader's Star Destroyer, the Dark Lord heard
of the activity on Hoth. "That's the system. And I'm sure
Skywalker is with them. Set your course and prepare your men."

The rebel evacuation had begun just in time. Imperial walkers were heading toward the base. As the first transports blasted into space, rebels on the ground began an attack. Troops fired cannons, and snowspeeders zoomed around the massive walkers, firing laser blasts. But the strong armor showed hardly a scratch.

Then Luke got an idea. "Use your harpoons and tow cables. Go for the legs. It might be our only chance of stopping them." Soon the tall legs of the walkers were immobilized in a web of cables. The walkers fell over and exploded, and the rebels were able to get away.

On board his X-wing fighter, Luke was explaining the course to his companion, R2. "We're heading for the Dagobah system."

Meanwhile, in the *Millennium Falcon,* Han, Leia, and Chewbacca were in trouble. Ships from the Empire were right behind them, and Han had done all he could to outrun them.

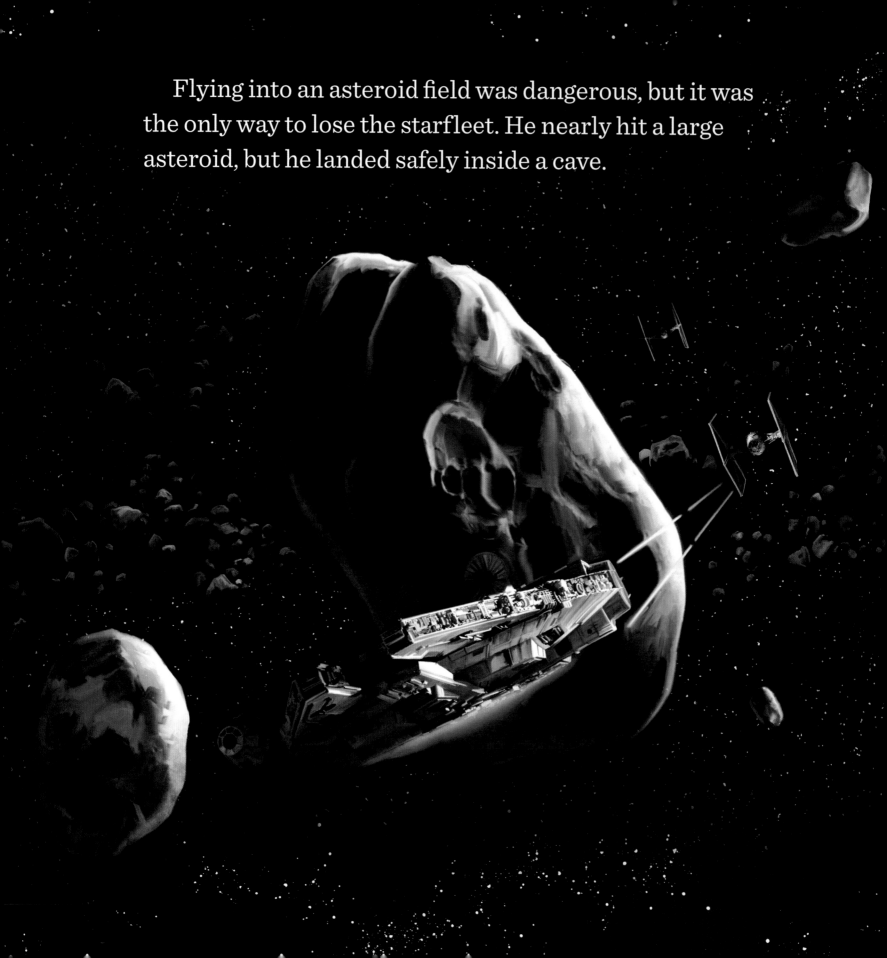

Flying into an asteroid field was dangerous, but it was the only way to lose the starfleet. He nearly hit a large asteroid, but he landed safely inside a cave.

On the other side of the galaxy, Luke crashed into the
swampy ground of Dagobah. This was not what he'd expected.
"Oh, Artoo, what are we doing here? It's like something out
of a dream."

Nearby, a creature spoke. "I am wondering, why are you here?"

"I'm looking for someone."

"Yoda. You seek Yoda. Take you to him, I will."

Luke followed. "Stay here and watch after the camp, Artoo."

Aboard his ship, Darth Vader knelt before the holographic image of the Emperor. "What is thy bidding, my master?"

"There is a great disturbance in the Force."

"I have felt it."

"The son of Skywalker must not become a Jedi."

"If he could be turned, he would become a powerful ally."

"Yes. Yes. He would be a great asset. Can it be done?"

"He will join us or die, my master."

Back on Dagobah, Luke discovered that his new friend was, in fact, Yoda the Jedi Master. But Luke had to convince the little creature that he was ready to become a Jedi Knight. After much discussion, Luke finally began the training. He learned how to sharpen his lightsaber skills, improve his balance and self-control, and increase his strength. Yoda was encouraged by what he saw.

"Remember, a Jedi's strength flows from the Force."

After flying out of a cave, Han piloted the *Millennium Falcon* to Cloud City for some minor repairs. An old friend, Lando Calrissian, met Han, Leia, and Chewbacca when they arrived, and gave them a tour of the city. When Lando showed them to the dining room, the group was met by Darth Vader. "We would be honored if you would join us." The bounty hunter Boba Fett was at his side.

Lando hung his head. "I'm sorry. They arrived right before you did."

On Dagobah, as Luke concentrated with the Force, he saw a vision of Cloud City. In it, he felt that Han and Leia were in danger.

"It is the future you see."

"Future? Will they die?"

"Difficult to see. Always in motion is the future."

"I've got to go to them." Luke began gathering his things.

Suddenly, Ben appeared. "It is you and your abilities the Emperor wants. That is why your friends are made to suffer."

Yoda became very serious. "Only a fully trained Jedi Knight with the Force as his ally will conquer Vader and his Emperor. If you end your training now, if you choose the quick and easy path, as Vader did, you will become an agent of evil. Strong is Vader. Mind what you have learned. Save you it can."

"I will. And I'll return. I promise." Then Luke climbed into his starfighter, fired up the engines, and flew away.

"Told you I did. Reckless is he. Now matters are worse."

Ben sighed. "That boy is our last hope."

"No, there is another."

Meanwhile, in a detention block on Cloud City, Han was thrown back into his cell with Leia and Chewbacca. "I feel terrible."

"Why are they doing this?"

Han was puzzled. "They never even asked me any questions."

The door to the cell opened again. It was Lando. He told them it was Luke the Dark Lord wanted. "Lord Vader has set a trap for him."

Leia was angry. "And we're the bait."

Lando turned to leave. "Well, he's on his way."

Later, in another part of the city, Darth Vader surveyed a carbon-freezing chamber with Lando. "This facility is crude, but it should be adequate to freeze Skywalker for his journey to the Emperor."

"Lord Vader, we only use this facility for carbon freezing. If you put him in there, it might kill him."

"Then we'll test it on Captain Solo first."

It wasn't long before Han and the others were brought into the chamber. Darth Vader looked at the doomed Han Solo. Chewbacca went crazy at the thought of his friend being put into carbon freeze.

"Chewie. The princess, you have to take care of her. You hear me?"

The Wookiee nodded.

Leia rushed over to Han. "I love you."

"I know."

Han was lowered into the pit, and within seconds, he was frozen and in perfect hibernation. "Reset the chamber for Skywalker. See to it that he finds his way in here."

At the same time, Luke had landed his ship in Cloud City and was looking for his friends. He'd heard a commotion and was hiding in a doorway as a procession of stormtroopers passed by. Suddenly, a laser blast narrowly missed his head. He'd been spotted! Dodging the laser fire, Luke ran for cover and ended up in a darkened chamber.

"The Force is strong with you, young Skywalker. But you are not a Jedi yet."

Luke was exactly where Darth Vader wanted him.

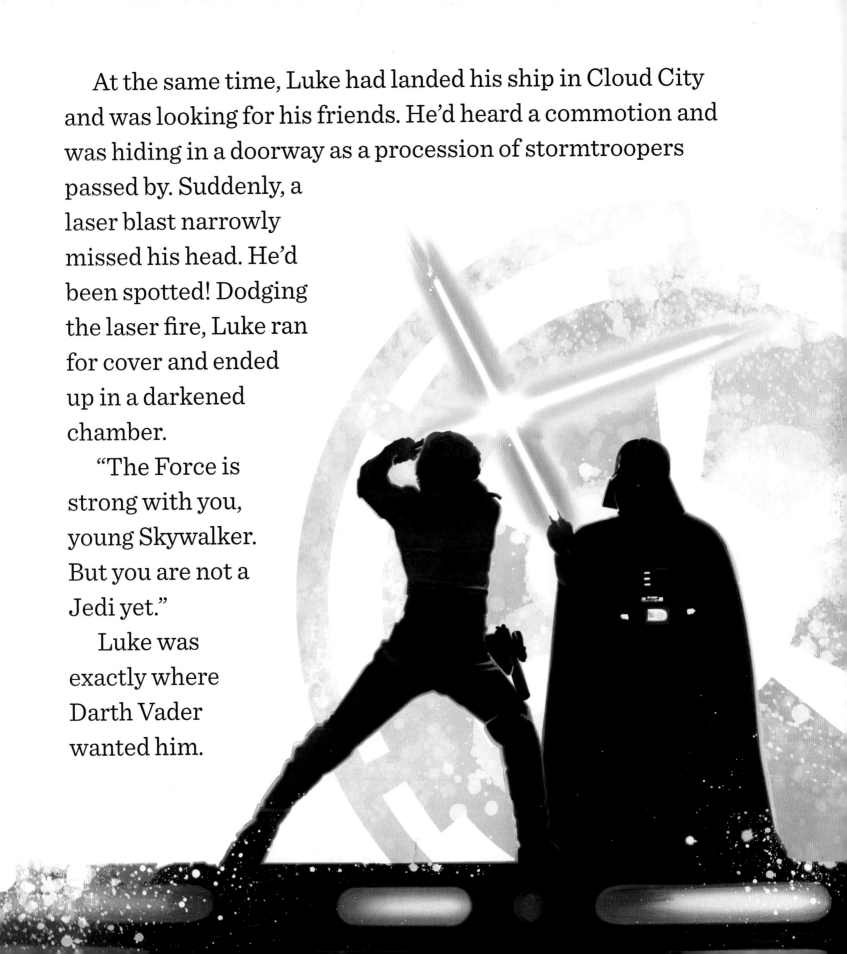

While the frozen Han was being taken away by Boba Fett, several stormtroopers escorted Lando and the others to Darth Vader's shuttle. Suddenly, they were surrounded by Cloud City guards. "Well done. Hold them in the security tower—and keep it quiet."

The first handcuffs that Lando unlocked were Chewbacca's. The Wookiee turned and began choking him. "There's still a chance to save Han . . . at the east platform."

Chewbacca and Leia raced after Han. But they were too late.

In the carbon-freezing chamber, Luke and Darth Vader were locked in combat. "Your destiny lies with me, Skywalker." Vader knocked Luke into the freezing pit. With a wave of his hand, the freezing equipment started to work.

With Jedi skill, Luke leaped out of the pit and stood before Vader.

"Obi-Wan has taught you well. You have controlled your fear. Now release your anger. Only your hatred can destroy me." Vader lunged at Luke, their sabers clashed, and Luke forced

Luke climbed down after Darth Vader and found himself in a small room. Vader sprang from the shadows. As they continued to fight, Vader used his powers to break heavy pieces of equipment off the wall and slam them into Luke. More and more things flew at the young Jedi, causing him to swing his lightsaber wildly. Vader stepped back. Then one piece of equipment crashed through a window, and suddenly, Luke was sucked out of the room and tossed onto a platform below.

At the same time, Leia and the others were racing through the city's corridors with stormtroopers at their heels. Lando paused at a communication terminal. "This is Lando Calrissian. The Empire has taken over the city. I advise everyone to leave before more Imperial troops arrive."

They ran down the landing platform and inside the *Millennium Falcon*. Chewbacca started the ship's engines. In a hail of laser fire, the ship tore off into the clouds.

Meanwhile, Luke crept along a ledge that stuck out over a huge bottomless reactor shaft. Suddenly, Vader was there. He forced the young Jedi down to the very end of the ledge. The crackle of swords echoed as Vader attacked Luke. In one swipe Luke lost his right hand—and his lightsaber—into the abyss below.

"There is no escape. Don't make me destroy you. Join me and I will complete your training. With our combined strength, we can end this destructive conflict and bring order to the galaxy."

Darth Vader towered over Luke. "If you only knew the power of the dark side. Obi-Wan never told you what happened to your father."

"He told me enough. He told me you killed him."

"No. I am your father."

"No! No! That's not true! That's impossible!"

"Luke. You can destroy the Emperor. It is your destiny. Join me, and together we can rule the galaxy as father and son."

Luke let go, falling away from his father, into the abyss.

He tumbled through the air until he landed on a vent hatch. The hatch opened and Luke fell out onto a weather vane. Try as he might, he couldn't get back to the hatch. As he dangled in space, he used the Force to call for help.

"Leia, Hear me! Leia!"

Far away, Leia felt very strange. "Luke. We've got to go back. I know where Luke is." Chewbacca turned the ship around. As they neared Luke's position, Lando harnessed himself to the emergency hatch and pulled Luke safely inside.

On board the medical ship, Luke had his arm fitted for a mechanical hand. Leia stood at the window watching Lando and Chewbacca in the cockpit of the *Millennium Falcon*. "Princess, we'll find Han. I promise."

Luke walked over to Leia as the *Millennium Falcon* zoomed into space.

The Empire had won this battle. But the rebels knew they would meet their enemy again someday. And maybe then they could continue the fight to bring freedom to the galaxy.

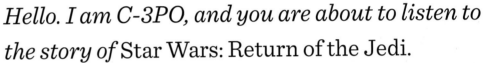

Hello. I am C-3PO, and you are about to listen to the story of Star Wars: Return of the Jedi.

You can also read along with the story in your book. Unless you are already programmed to know when the pages end, you will know it is time to turn the page when you hear this sound. . . .

I believe the storyteller is ready, so let us begin.

A long time ago in a galaxy far, far away. . . .

Read-Along Story Produced by Randy Thornton and Ted Kryczko;
Co-produced and Engineered by Jeff Sheridan; Adapted by Randy Thornton; Illustrated by Brian Rood.
℗ 2015 Walt Disney Records/Lucasfilm Ltd. © & ™ 2015 Lucasfilm Ltd. All rights reserved.

LUKE SKYWALKER HAD RETURNED HOME TO TATOOINE in an attempt to rescue his friend Han Solo from the clutches of the vile gangster Jabba the Hutt. Luke didn't know that the Galactic Empire had secretly begun construction on a new armored space station even more powerful than the dreaded Death Star. When completed, this ultimate weapon would spell certain doom for the small band of rebels struggling to restore freedom to the galaxy.

On board the new battle station, in a docking bay, Imperial troops stood nervously as Darth Vader's shuttle landed. The Dark Lord approached the commander. "I'm here to put you back on schedule."

"I tell you this station will be operational as planned."

"The Emperor does not share your appraisal of the situation."

"But he asks the impossible."

"Then perhaps you can tell him when he arrives."

"The Emperor is coming here? We shall double our efforts."

"I hope so, Commander. The Emperor is not as forgiving as I am."

On the desert planet Tatooine, C-3PO and R2-D2 had found the palace of Jabba the Hutt, where the frozen Han Solo was being held captive. As the droids stood before Jabba, R2 projected a message.

"I am Luke Skywalker, Jedi Knight and friend to Captain Solo. I seek an audience with Your Greatness to bargain for Han Solo's life. With your wisdom, I'm sure that we can work out an arrangement that will enable us to avoid any unpleasant confrontation."

Jabba growled his answer. There would be no bargain.

Moments later, a mysterious bounty hunter, pulling Chewbacca behind him in chains, approached Jabba's throne. Jabba gleefully paid the bounty on the Wookiee, then sent him to the dungeon.

That night, while everyone slept, the bounty hunter returned and went directly to Han's carbonite slab. He pressed a few buttons on its side, and Han was free of the carbonite. The bounty hunter was Leia!

"I've gotta get you out of here."

A curtain parted, and behind it were Jabba and his gang.

Now they were all prisoners. Han and Chewbacca were in the dungeon, and Leia was Jabba's servant. Suddenly, a dark figure appeared before Jabba. "I'm taking Captain Solo and his friends. You can either profit by this or be destroyed." It was Luke!

The gangster slammed his fist on a table, causing a trapdoor to open beneath the young Jedi. He fell into a filthy pit, where a monstrous creature stomped toward him. Luke dodged its attacks and finally crushed it under the heavy cell door. Jabba was furious!

Jabba then sentenced Luke and Han to die in the Pit of Carkoon, the nesting place of the terrifying carnivorous sand monster.

As Luke walked the plank over the pit, R2-D2 threw his lightsaber to him. The Jedi swung at his captors. Then Han and Lando battled the forces on their skiff while Luke rescued Leia. In a matter of moments, Jabba was dead, and our heroes were taking off in the *Millennium Falcon* to meet the rest of the Rebel Alliance.

Much later, Luke left the group and went off on his own to Dagobah. "I have a promise to keep—to an old friend."

When Luke arrived, he found that Yoda was very ill.

"No more training do you require. Already know that which you need. You must confront Vader. Then, only then, a Jedi will you be."

"Master Yoda . . . is Darth Vader my father?"

"Your father he is. Luke . . . there is . . . another . . . Sky . . . walker." The old Jedi Master closed his eyes and vanished.

As Luke prepared to leave, Ben Kenobi appeared.

"Obi-Wan! You told me Vader betrayed and murdered my father."

"Your father was seduced by the dark side of the Force. He ceased to be Anakin Skywalker and became Darth Vader."

"Yoda spoke of another."

"The other he spoke of is your twin sister."

"Leia. Leia's my sister."

"Bury your feelings deep down, Luke. They do you credit, but they could be made to serve the Emperor."

Luke returned to the rebel fleet and joined his friends in the main briefing room, where the plan of the attack was being outlined. One of the admirals announced that the Emperor himself was aboard the new Death Star, overseeing the final stages of the construction.

A strike force headed by General Han Solo would go to the moon of Endor to deactivate the energy shield that surrounded the battle station. At the same time, a group led by General Lando Calrissian would fly into the Death Star to blow up the main reactor.

The strike force landed on the moon of Endor. As they sneaked through its thick forest, they were spotted by a group of stormtroopers on speeder bikes. Luke and Leia jumped onto an available bike and took off. Zooming around the trees, Luke jumped from Leia's bike onto the back of a nearby stormtrooper's and pushed him off.

Suddenly, more stormtroopers raced up behind them. Luke went one way, Leia another. With a swing of his lightsaber, Luke cut the fins of one stormtrooper's bike and it went spinning into a tree.

Luke caught up with Han and found that Leia hadn't returned. They set out to look for her, but were caught in a trap set by the furry Ewoks.

When the Ewoks saw C-3PO, they thought he was a god. They escorted him and the others back to their village, where Leia was waiting. It was there that C-3PO told the Ewoks of our heroes' incredible adventure and their struggle against the Empire. The Ewoks declared our friends honorary members of their tribe and vowed to help in the battle against the Empire.

Seconds later, Leia followed Luke outside. "Luke, what's wrong?"

"Vader is here—now—on this moon. I have to face him."

"Why?"

"He's my father. . . . There's more. The Force is strong in my family. My father has it, I have it, and my sister has it. You are my sister."

Leia looked at her brother. "I know. Somehow I've always known. But why must you confront him?"

"Because there is good in him. I can save him."

Luke left and turned himself over to the Empire, where he was met by Darth Vader. "The Emperor has been expecting you."

"I know, Father."

"So you have accepted the truth."

"I have accepted that you were once Anakin Skywalker, my father."

"That name no longer has any meaning for me."

"Search your feelings, Father. You can't do this. I feel the conflict within you. Let go of your hate."

"It is too late for me, Son."

Lando led his fleet toward the
Death Star while Han, Leia,
and the Ewoks approached the
energy shield on Endor. At the
same time, Luke was brought
to the Emperor aboard the
battle station.

"Welcome, young
Skywalker. I've been
expecting you. Everything
that has transpired has done
so according to my design.
Your friends on Endor are
walking into a trap. As is
your rebel fleet."

Luke looked out
the window and saw
an entire legion
of Imperial Star
Destroyers waiting
for the rebels.

On Endor, the rebels couldn't make a move. Stormtroopers were all over them. "Freeze, you rebel scum." Suddenly, the stormtroopers were pelted with rocks and sticks as the Ewoks came out of their hiding places and attacked. The battle for Endor had begun.

Meanwhile, Lando and his group came out of hyperspace only to find the force field was still up and that Imperial TIE fighters were there waiting for them.

Back aboard the Death Star, the Emperor grinned at the young Jedi. "From here you will witness the destruction of the Alliance, and the end of your insignificant Rebellion."

Luke felt the dark side crawling within him. He controlled it as much as he could, but it was a tough struggle. His lightsaber was within reach. In a flash, it flew to his hand, and he swung at the Emperor. Vader's sword was there, instantly. The Emperor laughed maniacally as Luke's and Vader's swords clashed in a spray of sparks.

On Endor, the Ewoks were gaining ground as the battle wore on. Now there were Imperial scout walkers blasting and smashing their way through the forest. But the Ewoks ambushed the machines by tripping them with vines and crushing them with logs. Meanwhile, Han and Leia were trying to enter the bunker.

High above, Lando was leading an attack on the Imperial Star Destroyers until Han could get the shield down. But time was running out. He couldn't hold the Empire back for too much longer.

Aboard the Death Star, Vader searched for the young Skywalker, who had slipped into the shadows.

"You cannot hide forever, Luke. Give yourself to the dark side. It is the only way to save your friends. Your feelings for them are strong. Especially for—sister! So, you have a twin sister. If you will not turn to the dark side, then perhaps she will."

"No!" Luke went for Darth Vader, slashing wildly. He pounded the Dark Lord with his lightsaber, forcing him to the floor.

The Emperor laughed, and Luke suddenly realized what he had done. He tossed his weapon aside. "I'll never turn to the dark side. You failed, Your Highness. I am a Jedi, like my father before me."

"So be it, Jedi." The Emperor raised his hands. Bright blue bolts of electricity shot from his fingers and zapped Luke. "If you will not be turned, you will be destroyed." More energy struck Luke as he collapsed to the floor. Darth Vader struggled to his feet and stood beside his master.

Meanwhile, the rebels and the Ewoks managed to defeat the Imperial troops. They had placed several bombs in the control room, and in a matter of seconds, the entire shield generator had exploded.

Aboard the *Millennium Falcon*, Lando got word that the shield was down, so he restarted his attack run into the Death Star. Dodging the Imperial TIE fighters, Lando led the rebels through the superstructure and headed straight for the main reactor.

Back in his chamber, the Emperor glared at Luke twisting in pain on the floor. "Now, young Skywalker, you will die." Again, he blasted the Jedi Knight.

Vader looked at his doomed son and then at his master. Suddenly, Vader grabbed the Emperor from the back and lifted him over his head. The Emperor's energy bolts were now blasting Vader as he carried his master over to an open pit. With one final burst of strength, he hurled his evil ruler over the edge. Then the great warrior fell to the floor. Luke crawled to his father's side and pulled him to safety. They were both too weak to move.

Not far away, Lando and his team found the main reactor and fired at its supports. The massive structure began to collapse. Pursued by flames, the rebels headed for their escape route.

Inside the battle station, Luke dragged his father to the ramp of a shuttlecraft. "Luke, help me take this mask off."

Luke then removed his father's breath screen and looked at the man beneath the mask. "Now go, my son. Leave me."

"No. I can't leave you here. I've got to save you."

"You already have, Luke. You were right about me. Tell your sister . . . you were right." Anakin closed his eyes . . . and was gone.

After Luke pulled his father's armor aboard the shuttle, he lifted off from the docking bay. At that same moment, Lando, chased by flames, flew out of the Death Star. They both managed to escape just as the Death Star exploded in a giant fireball.

Back at the Ewok village, the rebels celebrated their victory over the Empire, while Luke set a torch to his father's armor. As the smoke rose overhead, X-wing fighters flew by, setting off fireworks in the sky. Elsewhere in the galaxy, there were similar celebrations going on.

Off on his own, Luke saw the ghostly images of Yoda, Ben, and his father smiling gratefully. The Jedi smiled back and rejoined his sister and friends.

At last, freedom had been restored to the galaxy.

A NEW HOPE

Narrator: **Chuck Riley**

Featuring the voice talents of:
C-3PO: **Anthony Daniels**
Princess Leia: **Pat Parris**
Darth Vader: **Brock Peters**
Uncle Owen: **Charles Howerton**
Luke Skywalker: **Joshua Fardon**
Obi-Wan Kenobi: **Roy Dotrice**
Han Solo: **Perry King**
Jabba the Hutt: **Randy Thornton**
Grand Moff Tarkin: **Tony Pope**

THE EMPIRE STRIKES BACK

Narrator: **Chuck Riley**

Featuring the voice talents of:
C-3PO: **Anthony Daniels**
Luke Skywalker: **Joshua Fardon**
Obi-Wan Kenobi: **Roy Dotrice**
Han Solo: **Perry King**
Darth Vader: **Brock Peters**
Yoda: **Corey Burton**
The Emperor: **Nick Tate**
Lando Calrissian: **Arye Gross**
Princess Leia: **Pat Parris**

RETURN OF THE JEDI

Narrator: **Chuck Riley**

Featuring the voice talents of:
C-3PO: **Anthony Daniels**
Darth Vader: **Brock Peters**
Commander Jerjerrod: **Charles Howerton**
Luke Skywalker: **Joshua Fardon**
Jabba the Hutt: **Randy Thornton**
Princess Leia: **Pat Parris**
Yoda: **Corey Burton**
Obi-Wan Kenobi: **Roy Dotrice**
The Emperor: **Nick Tate**
Imperial Commander: **Jeff Sheridan**
Anakin Skywalker: **Randy Thornton**

For information address Disney • Lucasfilm Press, 1101 Flower Street, Glendale, California 91201.

Printed in the United States of America.

First Edition, September 2015

1 3 5 7 9 10 8 6 4 2

FAC-038091-15240

ISBN 978-1-4847-3061-4

PRESS

Los Angeles • New York